MW01153559

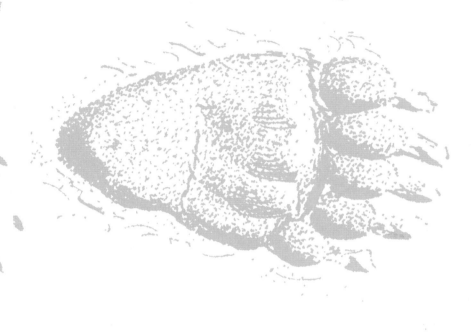

Searching for Grizzlies

by Ron Hirschi

Photographs by Thomas D. Mangelsen

Drawings by Deborah Cooper

Boyds Mills Press

Text copyright © 2005 by Ron Hirschi
Photographs copyright © 2005 by Thomas D. Mangelsen
Drawings copyright © 2005 by Boyds Mills Press, Inc.
All rights reserved.

Published by Boyds Mills Press, Inc.
A Highlights Company
815 Church Street
Honesdale, Pennsylvania 18431
Printed in China
Visit out Web site at www.boydsmillspress.com

Publisher Cataloging-in-Publication Data (U.S)

Hirschi, Ron.
    Searching for grizzlies / by Ron Hirschi ; photographs by
Thomas D. Mangelsen. —1st ed.
[ ] p. : col. photos. ; cm.
ISBN 1-59078-014-0
1. Grizzly bear. 2. Bears. 3. Endangered species.
I. Mangelsen, Thomas D. II. Title.
599.784 22   QL737.C27H57 2005

First edition, 2005
The text of this book is set in 13-point Wilke Roman.

10 9 8 7 6 5 4 3 2

ONCE, GRIZZLY BEARS ROAMED FREELY in most of the American West. Grizzlies hunted bison on the Great Plains. They even stalked elk and salmon along the rivers and ocean shores near what is now San Francisco. Today, they are gone from California and much of the rest of the United States.

Brrrr. Chilly morning in May. Fresh snow covers our tent, but bright yellow blossoms poke through a blanket of white on the hills above the camp. We can see a mom moose and calf munching willows just across the creek from our camp.

Greatly reduced in numbers, grizzlies live mainly in remote places, including some of our most beautiful wild lands. Yellowstone National Park and the surrounding mountains and valleys — "Greater" Yellowstone — is one of these few remaining natural areas.

We often go there, searching for bears.

GRIZZLY BEARS AWAKEN IN EARLY SPRING

from a winter sleep that might last four months or longer. They eat nothing during this time and lose one third or more of their body weight. Crawling out of her hibernation den, a bear sniffs the air in search of many kinds of foods to satisfy a winter's worth of hunger.

The day warms and the sun melts most of the snow that fell last night. We hike today along a trail leading up the creek into a broad valley. We pass through sweet-smelling sage-brush and groves of aspen with white bark and delicate dancing leaves that rustle in the wind. I photograph a small herd of elk, some with new calves. They look up, nervously. Are they startled by the sound of the camera shutter, or do they sense that a bear is nearby?

LIKE A TIGER SHARK SEARCHING FOR FISH,

lone grizzly bears stalk herds of elk, especially when calves are born in spring. Baby elk cannot run as fast as adults and often become prey of the swift and strong grizzly.

s getting late, but we start inking about going fishing ce we are back in camp. s good as a fresh-fish dinner sounds, here in Yellowstone we fish for fun, not for food. We catch and then release our fish with care so that bears, eagles, pelicans, and other predators can feast on the abundance of fat cutthroat trout.

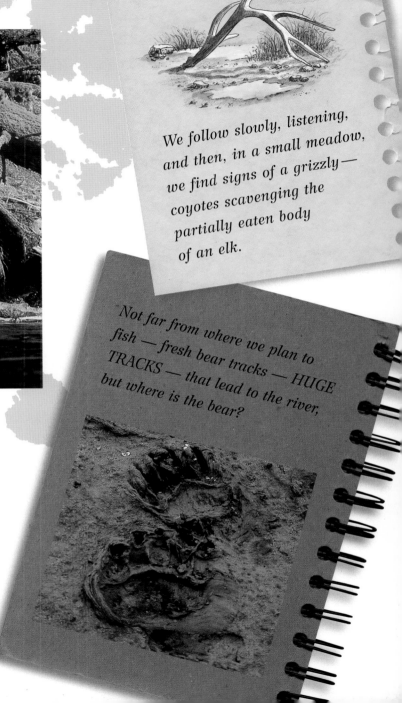

We follow slowly, listening, and then, in a small meadow, we find signs of a grizzly— coyotes scavenging the partially eaten body of an elk.

Not far from where we plan to fish — fresh bear tracks — HUGE TRACKS — that lead to the river, but where is the bear?

The bears search for other animals, too. They have an excellent sense of smell and follow the scent to find bodies of elk, deer, and bison that did not survive the harsh Rocky Mountain winter. These animals, known as winter kill, often fall through ice at the edges of lakes and rivers, where they become important parts of the early spring diet of Yellowstone bears.

GRIZZLY BEARS GROW TO AN ENORMOUS SIZE.

Largest of all land carnivores, an adult grizzly can be ten feet in length and reach weights well over a thousand pounds. The track of a grizzly is unmistakable — four-inch claws pressed into fresh snow or the ten-inch hind foot pressed into a muddy trail tells a hiker that a grizzly is near.

for fly rods and fine
Yellowstone cutthroat trout. All
the while, we watch over our
shoulders for any sign of bears. I
jump, hearing a splash, thinking
a bear hopes to swallow me for
dinner. It is only a trout,
swirling for big bugs. We choose
salmon flies, a special fishing
fly meant to imitate the
big-winged stoneflies. I soon
hook a two-pound trout, its
golden sides shimmering in the
last rays of the day's sun.

GRIZZLY BEARS HAVE ENORMOUS APPETITES,

but their food cycle begins with many small, even delicate, plants and animals. One of those cycles begins when leaves fall from trees and drop into the Yellowstone River.

First night in camp. Sleeping bags are rolled out and a big moon rises. There's just enough light to see shadows. Is that a bear? My heart races. Did a grizzly follow the trail we hiked after fishing? We had bear-proofed our camp, making sure food and gear were safely stowed. . . . So I drift into sleep, still thinking of those giant tracks while I listen to wolves howl from a ridge just beyond the Lamar River.

The sun is just peeking over the wolf's ridge. Mountain bluebirds rise and fall around us, dazzling the eye like little pieces of sky. They sing, "What Cheer! What Cheer!" Friendly birds, they let us take pictures up close until we pack a lunch to search for the bear who left its tracks nearby.

The leaves tumble and tear as they bounce through rocky rapids. Caddis flies living on the stream bottom gnaw the shredded leaves. In turn, the caddis is swallowed by a mayfly that is snatched by a larger predator, the stonefly. Hungry trout eat caddis and mayflies, but the spring swarms of stoneflies are a great feast for the fish. Grizzlies feast on the trout that ate the stonefly that swallowed the mayfly that chomped the caddis that shredded the leaf that fell from a tree growing on the bank of the river.

GRIZZLY BEARS HAVE EXCELLENT VISION. When hiking in bear country, it is safest to scan the distance and try to spot the bears before they see — or smell — you.

Grizzlies hunt elk by sight, but also sniff the air, trying to locate a herd with their keen sense of smell. They often have success bringing down both adult and calf elk while stalking them in the earliest and latest hours of day. Once a herd is located, the bear charges. Cows with calves often stand their ground, kicking with their sharp hooves as they try to protect themselves and their little ones. But lone elk and calves that wander away often become confused. Straying from the herd or from Mother may result in a chase like that between lion and zebra or cheetah and gazelle. Many elk then become a springtime meal for the hungry bear.

A FEW BEAR FACTS

Species: *Black Bear*
Length, Nose to Tail: *Usually about 5 1/2 feet*
Maximum Weight: *Just under 600 pounds*
Size at Birth: *8–12 ounces*
Color: *Black, cinnamon, and even white in some coastal British Columbia areas.*
Food: *Berries, ants, roots, ground squirrels, salmon, nuts, inner bark of trees*

Species: *Grizzly Bear (includes Alaskan Brown Bear)*
Length, Nose to Tail: *Can be up to 10 feet*
Maximum Weight: *Can reach 1,700 pounds, but usually from 330–1150 pounds*
Size at Birth: *1 pound*
Color: *Grizzled golden brown to black*
Food: *Carrion, moths, whitebark pine seeds, elk, deer, moose, many small animals, grass, berries, fish*

Species: *Polar Bear*
Length, Nose to Tail: *From 8 to 10 feet*
Maximum Weight: *Can be over 1,700 pounds, but averaging between 550–1,700 pounds*
Size at Birth: *1 to 2 pounds*
Color: *White*
Food: *Seals, walrus, fish, birds, whale carcasses, eggs, clams, crabs, seaweed, berries, mushrooms*

Second day of hiking. We startle a small black bear as we round a bend in the trail through the sage-brush. It is a beautiful glossy black, much different from many of the "brown" black bears we also see . . . the names of animals are sometimes confusing in that way. But no confusion between this black bear and a grizzly and we breathe easy. Still, we give the little bear lots of room. As we circle wide around it, the bear stares back at us, then goes on with its morning, sniffing the ground near a fallen tree.

BLACK BEARS ARE OFTEN MISTAKEN FOR GRIZZLIES.

For good reason. Black bears aren't always black. They are often the same golden brown as their much larger relatives. But the face of a grizzly is unmistakably larger, with ears that appear much smaller than those of a black bear. The shoulder hump of a grizzly also gives it a distinctive look, helping to separate it from a black bear, even from a great distance.

Black bear in focus. Click. The bear hears the camera. She stares. But she's more interested in dinner. She swats at an anthill then licks the ground, swallowing pine needles with each gob of insects.

Grizzly

Black Bear

BLACK BEAR MEALS INCLUDE ANTS and other insects as well as many kinds of plants. They also eat mice, birds, and other small animals. Black bears prey on far fewer large animals than the grizzly. Still, the black bear can and does stalk and kill calves as well as injured adult elk and deer.

Grizzly alert! An adult grizzly stands tall, staring in our direction. Luckily, we have been scouting the distant meadows and have stopped here, a safe ridgetop away. The bear is a female with two cubs. Mom bear looks unusually nervous. But the cubs appear to be aware of nothing but themselves. They tumble in tall grass, playing near their mother. Watching them, it is easy to see why people love stuffed bear toys. But we make no move to touch these baby bears . . . what would Mother do!

FEMALE GRIZZLIES ARE HIGHLY PROTECTIVE MOTHERS.
They give birth to sometimes one or three, but more often two cubs
while in the winter den. Baby grizzlies are about a foot long at birth
and are covered with such fine hair, they appear naked. In April or May,
mother bears lead their babies from the den when the cubs weigh about
ten pounds. She will keep her cubs with her through two winters,
giving birth about every other year.

Suddenly, a second adult grizzly appears. It's a lone male. The female charges him, then turns back to her cubs. She nudges them, scooting both babies up the hill in the opposite direction. She stands tall, charges again, chasing the much larger male through patches of snow and up, away from her little ones. The male's immense body ripples as he runs up the hill—straight to where we sit watching. From a safe distance?

GRIZZLIES ARE FIERCE PREDATORS.

Sometimes they kill others of their kind, especially cubs — perhaps the cubs fathered by another male. Biologically, this may be healthy for the male bear, increasing his chance to father offspring with females who have lost their young. Females fiercely defend their own young ones, but are known to kill other cubs, perhaps due to competition for food or feeding territories.

All is hushed. We don't move a single muscle as we watch the male. He stops often, looking over his massive shoulder at the female. She has stood her ground, and her cubs are a safe distance up the hill in the opposite direction. We close our eyes, hoping we are also safe as the male snorts a growl, breathing puffs of steamy breath all too close to our perch atop a smooth granite boulder. I open, then close my journal. I want to draw his face, his rising plume of steamy breath.

But we hug the rock and hold our breath as the huge bear walks past, then disappears beyond the ridge behind us. The female drops down and returns to her cubs. She soon gathers them close. The babies nurse in the open. Have they learned a lesson in how to avoid danger? Or is mother bear so good at protecting them, they never even knew why they were chased up the mountain?

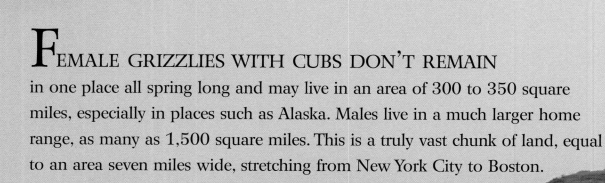

FEMALE GRIZZLIES WITH CUBS DON'T REMAIN

in one place all spring long and may live in an area of 300 to 350 square miles, especially in places such as Alaska. Males live in a much larger home range, as many as 1,500 square miles. This is a truly vast chunk of land, equal to an area seven miles wide, stretching from New York City to Boston.

Grizzlies avoid one another's company except for mating. This is not true in coastal Alaska, where many brown bears (as grizzlies are called there and in much of western Canada) gather to feast on salmon that return to rivers to complete their life cycle. With an abundance of salmon in the cold, clear rivers, Alaskan bears often stand close to one another, even near mother bears with cubs on their first fishing expedition, as they all prey on the fish.

GRIZZLY BEARS ARE ABLE TO DIG DEEP with help from their long and strong claws. As winter approaches, they dig to expand or create a hibernation den. They also dig for tender roots and small mammals. In late fall, they often roam high in the mountains of Yellowstone to search the edge of a special forest. Here, they dig to find a tasty stash of whitebark pine seeds hidden by squirrels or birds. Grizzlies also scrape and dig large holes to cover leftover meals, sometimes burying their prey several feet deep.

Night has fallen. When daylight faded, our view of the mother bear and her cubs also vanished as shadows and shapes melted into darkness. Alert for any sounds of the lone male, we hike down the mountain to camp. Each snap in the brush causes us to stop. But during the three-mile walk back to dinner and the warmth of our campfire, we soon begin to enjoy the many sounds of a Yellowstone evening. Entering a clearing, we can just see . . .

the outline of a skilled hunter of the night — a great gray owl. The owl drops from its perch on wings as silent as the soft wind brushing against our faces. We breathe its freshness deeply, happy to be in such rare and beautiful company.

EACH SEASON HAS ITS special demands on the grizzly bear. Mother grizzlies have the extra demand of nursing and finding adequate food for her cubs. As fall approaches, all the bears of the Greater Yellowstone need to find a safe den site.

THEY ALSO MUST
fatten up for the long winter
sleep ahead. Some bears might
find plentiful fish supplies, but
others turn to an unusual food
source. They feed on moths as the
fuzzy insects fly up to alpine
meadows to sip flower nectar. It
takes a lot of insects to fill a grizzly
belly, and a single bear has been
known to swallow as many as forty
thousand moths in just one day.

No MATTER WHAT MEAL
they search for, grizzly bears hunt for
food and shelter in a far smaller
homeland than in times past.
Highways, towns, and ranches stretch
in all directions beyond Yellowstone —
lands covering several states where
bears are not welcome and where
grizzly bear food supplies are no
longer abundant.

You might visit the Greater Yellowstone, including Yellowstone and Grand Teton National Parks, to search for bears that do have a home. Search from a safe distance in springtime along rivers and streams, up high ridgetops, or in mountain meadows, where you might find these great grizzly bears waking from their long winter naps.

NOTE

THIS BOOK FIRST CAME TO LIFE on a ridgetop not far from Dunraven Pass in Yellowstone National Park. I was taking notes as a mother grizzly chased a male away from her two cubs, protecting them from danger. Later that day, I thumbed through my tattered journal. Here and there, my handwriting got all scribbly. The notes showed my excitement at each grizzly encounter. There was the sketch of two guys running as I took note of the bear who walked down to the banks of Slough Creek one evening, just as my friend Mike Harris and I stopped fishing cutthroat. Our hike back to camp included constant looks over our shoulders because the bear had seen us and was no more than half a soccer field away when we turned away from the creek.

While I combined many other experiences in the book, Tom Mangelsen includes still more. I am lucky to get to work with Tom, one of the world's best nature photographers. Tom lives and works in The Greater Yellowstone and has spent much more time than I with bears. His photographs show you much about their way of life and their homeland. His images also help to show the beauty of wildlife and wild places.

Tom and I both hope you enjoy this book. More importantly, we hope you get a chance one day soon to visit Yellowstone, Grand Teton, Glacier, or others of our western National Parks. Also, take the time to get to know more about bears and other predators who need lands even more vast than those set aside inside the parks.

Our world changes quickly, and sometimes people don't protect enough habitat for wildlife as those changes take place. This is especially true for predators since they require so much space and so many prey animals to support their needs. As you can easily guess, grizzly bears don't read maps. They know nothing about boundary lines we place around our national parks.

Bears, wolves, cougars, and many other animals move in and out of the parks. They need to move freely. If allowed the space, they will also move back into home-lands where they once lived, well beyond the borders of the parks. That is why many people call for protection of an ever-widening circle beyond our parks, the "Greater" Yellowstone — lands vast enough to make future homes for the great grizzly bears.